The Squirrel Manifesto

A bushy tale for finding happiness

Written by
Ric Edelman and Jean Edelman

Illustrated by
Dave Zaboski

ALADDIN
New York London Toronto Sydney New Dehli

ALADDIN | An imprint of Simon & Schuster Children's Publishing Division
1230 Avenue of the Americas, New York, New York 10020
First Aladdin hardcover edition November 2018
Copyright © 2018 by Ric Edelman, Jean Edelman and Dave Zaboski
All rights reserved, including the right of reproduction in whole or in part in any form.
ALADDIN and related logo are registered trademarks of Simon & Schuster, Inc.
For information about special discounts for bulk purchases, please contact
Simon & Schuster Special Sales at 1-866-506-1949 or business@simonandschuster.com.
The Simon & Schuster Speakers Bureau can bring authors to your live event.
For more information or to book an event contact the Simon & Schuster
Speakers Bureau at 1-866-248-3049 or visit our website at www.simonspeakers.com.
Book designed by Dave Zaboski
The text of this book was set in Nanami HM and Neutraface Text.
Manufactured in China 0918 SCP
10 9 8 7 6 5 4 3 2 1
Library of Congress Control Number 2018948561
ISBN 978-1-5344-4166-8 (hc)
ISBN 978-1-5344-4167-5 (eBook)

To Lucy
and all the young children
who have graced our lives

There is a forest
not too far from here,

where the warm winds blow
for most of the year.

It's in this fine place
you'll learn something good,

from some critters who live
in the Walkabout Wood.

It is a land alive
with infinite hues,

a symphony of colors
in reds, yellows, and blues.

Where animals come,
and animals go,

with hardly a care
for Michelangelo.

From dawn to dusk,
and dusk to dawn,

each awakens with joy
and goes to sleep with a yawn.

And while I may be small,
perhaps you've heard,

my name is Wren,
and I'm your guide bird!

I usually share,
in songs, not in words,

every little thing in the
language of birds.

I know the secrets of
every herd, hive, and clan.

I watch with care
as they work, live, and plan.

The ants are fastidious,
disciplined, and true,

the beavers industrious,
and the foxes shrewd.

And of all the animals,
from the cliffs to the sea,

there's one crazy bunch
who knows how to be!

Oh! They frolic and play
and seem without a care,

but they know a secret
I'm emboldened to share.

It is a singular truth
I noticed from above,

how these creatures live
with vision, charity, and love.

I witnessed Olde Walden,
who lives in the Big Tree,

teach some young 'uns
how to gather and live free.

"Come with me!" he cried.
"Let's leap and let's scramble,

from tree limb to treetop
and down to the bramble.

And I'll teach you some things
you'll always remember,

from season to season,
September to September:

To gather is great!
A squirrel digs and he seeks,

but don't hoard too much—
it won't fit in your cheeks.

This land is our home,
these valleys and streams.

We owe it our lives,
our future, our dreams.

Some of our boon
goes back to the glade,

so there's always a place
for more young 'uns to shade.

We honor the past
and what's been done,

and tend to the present
for what it will become.

Next we take some nuts
and we squirrel them away,

so we have something
for a cold, rainy day.

If we save just a little,
a couple nuts at a time,

it leads to what matters:
Squirrel Peace of Mind.

Next we honor ourselves
with the gains that we earn.

We deserve a good life,
so we enjoy our own turn.

We put some of our flow
back into the stream,

to add to the current
and live what we dream.

And lastly, I urge you,
to others give back.

It is hard in this forest
for all those who lack.

Your life is a blessing
of gifts precious and rare.

You multiply the grace
when you care and you share.

The old squirrel looked up,
and then he said, "Presto!

We live by these words—
it's the Squirrel Manifesto!"

Care for the world
You live in, and act.
Save a little.
Spend a little.
And always
give back!

Olde Walden then granted
that I share this with you.

so when you gather your nuts,
you'll know what to do.

And if you ever forget,
just look to the trees,

and remember the squirrels
who live there with ease!

The Squirrel Manifesto Guide for Grown-Ups

Financial habits form early. Children learn by observing your behavior and through their own experiences. That's why it's important to make sure your children are treating money the right way. From allowances and birthday money to cash they'll one day earn babysitting or mowing lawns, the Squirrel Manifesto provides the platform to set your children on the path to a lifetime of fiscal responsibility.

1. Tax a little. Children need to be taught from a very early age that they don't get to keep everything they earn. Just as the government collects a third of your income in taxes, you should withhold one-third of your child's allowance, birthday money, or babysitting earnings. Call it a tax to get the child used to the fact that they can't keep everything they earn—allowing them to adjust their spending and saving plans accordingly. Then, without the child's knowledge, put the "taxes" into a savings or investment account. Then, when your child is ready to buy a car or go to college, hand over the account. Not only will your child think you're a hero, but they'll also learn the value of delayed gratification and long-term investing!

2. Spend a little. The benefit of earning or receiving money is the joy of spending it. Allow your child to buy whatever he or she wants—a comic book, toy, candy (purchases always subject to your approval, of course!)—so the child can develop a positive relationship with money by experiencing the enjoyment that using money can bring.

3. Save a little. Not every item the child wants can be purchased immediately, for some items simply cost more than the child has available to spend. So, if your child wants a video game, bicycle, smartphone—or a car or college—have him or her set aside some money. By training the child to save long-term for big goals, you'll be teaching the benefit of delayed gratification and arming them with the skills they need to avoid impulse buying.

4. Give a little. Children need to be taught that the opportunities that come with money are also imbued with the responsibility and obligation to serve those who are less fortunate. For every dollar your child receives, decide on a portion that will go to philanthropy. The amount should be consistent, meaning that every time the child receives or earns money, the same percentage is set aside for this purpose. The percentage must be material to reflect true sacrifice and service. Let the child decide who receives the money, whether it's a church, a charity, or a friend in need, and in the process he or she will discover that the greatest joy in spending comes not from spending on themselves but on supporting and caring for others.

By teaching your kids the Squirrel Manifesto, you can help them form positive financial habits that will last their entire lives.

RIC EDELMAN is widely regarded as one of the nation's top financial advisors. He was ranked #11 on the 2017 list of the nation's Top Wealth Advisors by *Forbes*[1] and previously ranked three times as the nation's #1 Independent Financial Advisor by *Barron's*.[2] In 2017 Ric received a lifetime achievement award from the International Association of Registered Financial Consultants.[3] He is an inductee of *Research* magazine's Financial Advisor Hall of Fame[4] and has been named among the fifteen most transformative people in the industry by *InvestmentNews*[5] and one of the investment advisory field's ten most influential figures by *RIABiz*.[6] Ric is also a #1 *New York Times* bestselling author who has written nine books on personal finance.

While Ric emphasizes the more traditional elements of personal finance, Jean shares her insight to help us see ourselves and the world around us in a positive, loving way. Her book, *The Other Side of Money*, is a compilation of her writings over the last two decades. It asks the questions: What are we doing to make our lives rich and fulfilling? Are we tuned in to the people in our lives? Do we treat each other with respect? Are we taking care of our local environment and resources?

JEAN EDELMAN serves on several corporate and nonprofit boards, including Rowan University, where she graduated with a degree in home economics, consumer economics, marketing, and nutrition. As a Rowan undergrad, Jean was the first female president of the Student Government Association and recipient of the Distinguished Senior Award. She was named Alumnus of the Year in 1994.

Jean and Ric are benefactors of the Inova Edelman Center for Nursing at Inova Health Foundation, the Edelman Planetarium, and Edelman Fossil Park—both at Rowan University. They also actively support Boys & Girls Clubs, Northern Virginia Therapeutic Riding, and many other charities.

Jean and Ric are the founders of Edelman Financial Services, which in 2018 joined forces with Financial Engines to create the nation's largest Registered Investment Advisor. With combined assets under management of nearly $200 billion, the combined organization serves consumers via their 401(k) plans at work and provides financial planning via local offices coast-to-coast.

Ric and Jean with Summer and Vicki

EDELMAN
FINANCIAL SERVICES
LLC

Financial
Engines®

DAVE ZABOSKI is a classically trained painter, illustrator, and former Senior Animator with Disney, Sony, and Warner Bros. He has drawn for such classic films as *Beauty and the Beast, Aladdin, The Lion King, Pocahontas, The Hunchback of Notre Dame, Hercules, Tarzan, The Emperor's New Groove, Fantasia 2000,* and more.

Along with this latest offering, he has co-created several children's books including *Gideon's Dream,* with Ken Dychtwald, PhD, and Maddy Dychtwald, and *You with the Stars in Your Eyes,* with Deepak Chopra. He has been the expedition artist on a search for a lost temple in the Andes, was the West Coast Champion of Art Battles (a gladiatorial art competition between street artists for live painting supremacy), and has painted for the Dalai Lama.

He is a sought-after and entertaining public speaker who has taught collaborative creativity to entrepreneurs, educators, artists, and others at world-renowned centers like Esalen, Summit, the Chopra Center, and Rancho La Puerta, among others. Dave is on the faculty of Singularity University and the headmaster at Lucid University.

He speaks often about the necessity for technology to multiply compassion and consults with creative teams on building collaborative cultures. Dave lives on a ranchette in Southern California with his wife and daughter, along with a small menagerie of four-legged friends.
